RAINBOW MOMENTS

Written & illustrated by Nikki Rogers

Have you ever heard God speak to you
and tell you of His love?
Or remind you of His promises
and that His grace is enough?

God gave Noah a rainbow,
and promised that He would
never flood the earth again
and showed him He is good.

God gives special rainbow moments
to speak to me and you,
to remind us of his promises
and the great plans He has too!

You may find a four-leafed clover
and hear God say He's very proud,
He sees you and has picked you out
from amongst a great big crowd.

God can speak to you through people
who have just the words to say
to encourage you and lift you up
and help you through the day.

Maybe you have found a coin
and even though it's small,
it reminded you that God provides
and you need not worry at all.

When you read you may hear Him
speaking softly to your heart,
that He's always with you
and He has been from the start.

Joshua 1:9

God may send you a feather
saying "You can do all things",
and as you wait and trust in Him
you'll rise as if on wings.

God shows you pretty flowers,
although some day they will fade,
He created you more beautiful.
You are wonderfully made.

When you hear the sweetest sound
of birds singing songs for you,
let your heart hear God's voice
as He sings over you too.

Take a moment to breathe in deep,
feel the warming of the sun,
think of God's great love for you
and all the good things He has done.

He reminds us of His promises
and we're special in His eyes.
His plans for us are always good,
His love greater than the skies.

For He has not forgotten
and He hears us when we pray,
God is faithful and His mercies
are new for us each day.

If you take time to stop and listen,
look and you will see
the precious rainbow moments
that God sends for you and me.

Written with love for my wonderful church family.
Inspired by the beautiful Elizabeth Galo.
May we continue to encourage and remind each other of
God's amazing love & exceeding great & precious promises.

For more info, **lesson plans & FREE resources** visit
www.createdtobe.com.au
All books are also available as eBooks
Like us at www.facebook.com/created.to.be.you

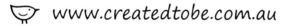

Discover more titles by Nikki Rogers

A Beautiful Girl is a lovely book that celebrates the diversity in every girl. With beautiful illustrations accompanied by poetry, little girls and big girls will love this book that inspires them to shine the beauty within.

A Hero Is explores the characteristics of what makes a hero and just how diverse heroes can be. With vibrant illustrations accompanied by poetry this book will inspire little boys to be heroes in their everyday life.

The Garden In My Heart is a beautifully illustrated book about sowing and reaping that encourages children to sow good things in their heart. We all have a garden that can produce flowers of joy or weeds of jealousy and bitterness.

Rainbow Moments is a colorful book that explores the many different ways that God can speak to us. It encourages the reader to stop, look, listen and recognize the special moments when God reminds us of His love and promises.

Made in the USA
San Bernardino, CA
06 December 2014